MR. CEOOOOOOOO

OLIVIA T. TURNER

www.OliviaTTurner.com

Edited by Karen Collins Editing
Cover Design by Olivia T. Turner

BECOME OBSESSED WITH OTT

Sign up to my mailing list for all the latest OTT news and get a free book that you can't find anywhere else!

OBSESSED
By Olivia T. Turner
A Mailing List Exclusive!

When the rich and powerful CEO Luke Gray looks out his

office window and sees an angel working in the next building, he buys the entire company just to be near her.

But what Zoe is going to find out is that this obsessed and possessive man will not only own her company, but he'll own her too.

Go to www.OliviaTTurner.com to get your free ebook of Obsessed

"It's time to get a taste of what I'm paying for."

One look at her walking through the halls of my office has me hooked.

She's my new secretary and she'll have to obey my *every* command.

Follow my strict dress code.

And there's no *experience* required, in fact, her inexperience is preferred.

Because I'm going to show her how a real alpha boss does it.

I'm going to show her why they call me Mr. CEOooooooo.

You down with OTT? This is an Olivia T. Turner book, which means it features a possessive and totally obsessed Over The Top alpha male who isn't afraid to take what he wants! If you like your book boyfriends sweet and cuddly than shut the computer off and walk away. If you like your heroes, rough, dirty and possessive to the extreme, come on in and have some fun...

For the real Mr. Decker.
I would have fucked you, if you would have asked.

1

"Miss Martin," the woman says, watching me with a tightness in her eyes. She looks like someone who doesn't like to have her time wasted, and she thinks that's exactly what I'm going to do.

I wish she wasn't right.

"Present," I say, raising my hand as I stand up. *Present? Are you fucking kidding me, Violet?*

It's bad enough that I look like I'm straight out of high school (which I am), but do I have to act like it too?

The woman just rolls her eyes before turning and walking away. I grab my father's old briefcase, which is currently empty, and hurry after her.

"Good luck," the receptionist says, smiling at me as I rush past her.

"Thanks," I answer with a gulp. I'm going to need it.

It's my first job interview and I have no idea what I'm doing. All I know about this company is the name. *Decker Engineering.*

I'm not even supposed to be here. My mother applied for this job for herself, but when she couldn't get out of bed this morning, I threw on her clothes, grabbed my dad's old brief-case (one of the few things he left us besides all of his debt), and came myself.

I'm sick of having the landlord stopping me in the hallway to remind me that we're three months late on rent and that there are 'other ways' of paying him back, I'm sick of having to shoplift at the grocery store, I'm sick of wearing socks that look like Swiss cheese, but more than anything, I'm sick of feeling like exactly what my dad said we were before he split: worthless.

I refuse to prove him right.

The office is beautiful with old thick beams running along the high ceilings. Everybody is dressed so well, and I feel so out of place in my faded black skirt and blouse that's way too tight.

My stomach is filled with butterflies as I walk down the hallway and look out the wall of windows. We're on the forty-second floor and the view of Chicago is incredible from up here. Everything is incredible in here. Even the carpet under my feet is so thick and soft that it makes me want to curl up under a desk and sleep on it.

The woman never looks back as she power walks down the hall, probably hoping that I got lost a few turns ago, and decided to go back home. I would love to slink out of this place that I don't fit into at all, but desperation makes me stay.

We turn around another corner of offices before walking past a large conference room where there's a meeting going on. A man is standing at the head of the huge table, talking to about a dozen people who are all listening intently to him. I try to keep my eyes on my scuffed-up shoes as I walk past, but I feel eyes on me and I have a sudden urge to look up.

The man at the head of the table is staring right at me with hard intense eyes. A warm shiver flows through me as I look at his strong jaw that's covered in the perfect amount of stubble. His hair is slicked to the side, every hair meticulously in place like he controls everything, even the individual hairs on his head.

The butterflies in my stomach really start to go nuts as I wonder why he's staring at me like that. My heart starts pounding when I realize that he's not talking anymore. The meeting is on hold as I walk past the room.

He's wondering why an impostor is walking down the halls of his kingdom. He's pissed that I'm here.

His eyes follow me as I walk, his neck turning like a swivel on his frozen body. My cheeks are so hot that I'm worried the sprinklers in the ceiling are going to go off and give us all a shower.

He must be the boss. Authority and power radiate from every pore in his body. I can feel it even though we're not even in the same room. His thick and muscular body just exudes control and dominance. His fitted suit looks painted on his large frame, hugging his round arms and making me swallow hard. My eyes flit to the tattoo on the back of his hand that's sexy as fuck. He doesn't look like what I consider the corporate type, but then again, I don't know anything about this world. I just graduated high school a few months ago.

He disappears from my view when I pass the room and an immediate sense of loss hits my core like a punch in the stomach.

"Let's go, *Miss* Martin," the woman says, staring at me with narrow eyes. "I have other interviews to get through, and I want to get *this one* over with quickly."

My cheeks get even redder as I lower my head and

follow her. She opens the door to her office and gives me a cold smile as she lets me in.

Nausea creeps up my throat as I take a seat in the plush leather chair in front of her desk. She shakes her head as she closes the door, cursing something under her breath that I can't hear. Not going to lie, I'm pretty glad that I don't hear it.

"Well, this is interesting," she says, looking over my mother's resume as she walks around the desk and sits down. "Ten years experience as a cashier. Six years working as a waitress in a diner. Tell me Miss Martin. Did you start working when you were in diapers?"

My body slinks down in the chair as her hard eyes dart to mine, narrowing viciously. My mother is supposed to be sitting in this chair, not me.

But she's been suffering from severe depression since my father left last year, and some days she just can't get herself out of bed. Today was one of those days.

I decided to take her place and do what my grandfather always used to say: Fake it till you make it. Although, right now I think they should change that to: Fake it till you throw up.

"I think you might have the wrong resume," I say, swallowing hard as I grab my briefcase and put in on my lap. I laugh nervously as I force open the rusted latch that always sticks, and open it up. "I think I have another one in here somewhere."

She can't see inside so I pretend like I'm ruffling through important papers when all I'm doing is clearing the cobwebs in the empty old briefcase.

"What's your real name?" she asks, not buying my little routine.

"Violet Martin," I answer, slowly closing the briefcase as I look up at her.

"Why are you wasting my time, Violet?" she asks as she leans back in the chair and crosses her arms. She doesn't look happy. She has heavy bags under her eyes and looks like she hasn't been laid in a while. There's a framed photo of two dogs on her desk, but no picture of a husband or boyfriend in sight. Maybe if she smiled more, she would get one.

"I apologize for the mix-up, Mrs—?"

I wait for her to fill in her name, but she just glares at me, letting me sit there uncomfortably.

"I may not have a ton of experience," I say.

"Or any experience," she mutters.

"Or *any* experience," I continue. "But I'm a very hard worker, and I'll show up on time every day."

She uncrosses her arms and leans forward. She smells like the old stinky potpourri that my grandmother used to have. "This is a Fortune 500 company," she says like I'm supposed to know what that means. "We're the top engineering firm in the Midwestern United States. Top five in the country. Top twenty in the world. We've built some of the most recognizable buildings and structures in the world, from the Al Bashshar Tower in Dubai, to the Imperial Square in London, to the Ola Falante Portugues Soccer Stadium in Brazil. We require a bit more than punctuality when acquiring a job applicant."

"I have a briefcase," I say, laughing nervously as I lift it up, showing her the frayed corner.

She doesn't find my sense of humor amusing.

"Thank you for coming in and wasting my time, Violet," she says as she crumples my mother's resume up into a ball and tosses across the office at the garbage can. I'm secretly thrilled when she misses.

"Actually," I say, starting to panic as she gets up. "It was my mother who was supposed to come."

"And she sent you," she says, sneering at me. "How lovely."

"Do you think we can reschedule her for tomorrow?" I ask, already knowing the answer. "She would make a *great* office assistant."

The woman laughs. Well, it's more like a sad snicker than a laugh. "I think we know all we need to know about you and your *mother*. We'll call you if we're interested."

All of the energy gets zapped from my body as she stands up. My legs are weak and there's a pain in my chest as my heartbeat turns sluggish. I close my eyes, fighting back the burning tears that are desperately trying to burst out.

Don't cry in front of her. Please, don't cry in front of her.

"Perhaps the homeless shelter down the street would be more suited to you," she says, enjoying watching me squirm.

"Are they hiring?" I ask, raising my eyebrows in hope.

She chuckles. "It's time to go, Violet."

I take a deep breath and stand up when the door swings open, making me gasp. The man from the conference room-the fierce looking one with the tattooed hand—bursts in, locking his dark eyes on me.

The hairs on the back of my neck raise as I look up at him in surprise. He's massive. I thought he looked big in the conference room, but he looks absolutely giant standing over me in the small office.

His jaw is clenched as he stares down at me with heated eyes. He looks agitated, or pissed, I can't tell which. He's breathing in short violent gasps, and I'd bet his heart is beating even harder than mine is.

"Mr. Decker," my interviewer slash tormentor says, straightening up as she looks at him. He doesn't even glance at her.

"I'll finish her interview in *my* office," he says in a firm dominant voice that sends a shiver racing through my trembling body.

"I don't think that's necessary, Mr. Decker," the woman says, waving a dismissive hand at me. "She's not experienced enough, and I don't think she'd be a proper fit."

He looks annoyed as he pries his eyes off of me and turns to her like he's upset that she's making him look anywhere else but at my tingling body.

"I'll bring her to my office, and see if she's a *proper fit*." His eyes fall down to my skirt as he says the last two words, and my pussy pulses in response.

It sounded so sexual, but it was probably just in my head. *And* between my legs.

"Mr. Decker," the woman says, not knowing when to shut up. "She has no experience."

"Perfect," he whispers, licking his lips as he stares at me like he's a hungry wolf about to chow down on a baby lamb. "I like them untouched and inexperienced."

There's a flutter in my chest as it gets incredibly hot in the small office.

The woman is desperate to get me out of this building. She grabs a handful of resumes off the table and thrusts them at him. "Here are twenty more qualified candidates that would be more than—"

"Carol," he snaps, turning to her with a look that makes her take a step back. His thick neck is strained tight and turning red. He grabs my arm in a possessive grip, holding me like he's never going to let me go. "I want *her*."

Carol doesn't look so tough anymore as she nods up and down quickly with her mouth closed in a pinched line.

Without another word, he pulls me out of the office, squeezing my bicep with his powerful tattooed hand.

It's immature and exactly what Carol would expect of me, but I don't care. I stick my tongue out at her as we leave.

The man is acting like a barbarian in a designer suit as he pulls me down the hall so fast that I have to run to keep up. I'm sure if I fall he would just keep dragging me.

"Mr. Decker," someone says, popping his head out of an office that we pass. "Can I get your signa—"

"*Later*," he growls, practically snarling at the guy. The guy's face drops in shock as he turns from Mr. Decker to me.

Mr. Decker doesn't slow one step as he charges past the office, pulling me along with him.

I swallow hard as we arrive at a huge corner office that's bigger than the apartment I live in. There's an older woman who looks like she's about to retire who's sitting at a large desk outside. I think she's his personal secretary.

She holds out a post-it note when she sees him coming. "Mr. Xi called and is ready to finally close the deal," she says, looking thrilled to give the boss some good news.

He just barrels past her and opens his door. "Hold all of my calls," he grunts as he pulls me into the office. "Make sure we're not disturbed."

I swallow hard as he slams the door closed and races to the blinds that are hanging over the huge windows that look out into the office.

"Sit," he orders as he closes each one of them.

My pulse races as I see the secretary's shocked face disappear behind a closed blind.

I sit in a chair in front of his massive desk, trying not to look as nervous as I feel.

When the door is locked, the blinds are closed, and he's satisfied that no one can see in, he slowly takes off his jacket and folds it on the black leather couch along the wall. My breath is trapped in my throat as I watch him slowly and meticulously roll his sleeves up his thick tattooed forearms one at a time.

"Now," he says in a smooth controlled voice as he walks over to the desk in front of me and leans against it. "The *real* interview will begin."

I gulp when I glance down and see his rock hard cock jutting out against the inside of his fitted pants.

"And," he says, looking down at my pussy that's getting wetter by the second, "we'll find out if you are a *proper fit.*"

2

MY COCK IS SO HARD THAT IT'S ACHING AS I LOOK DOWN AT the pretty little blonde squirming in the chair in front of me. She's looking up at me under her long eyelashes with these big brown doe-like eyes that are making me crazy.

"How old are you, Bambi?" I ask in a voice that's deeper than normal. The name just kind of slips out, but it suits her perfectly.

If she's a helpless young fawn than I must be the hunter. That's pretty damn fitting too.

"Twenty-two," she says, shifting in her chair as she answers. She's a shitty liar.

"Okay, eighteen," she answers quickly when she sees that I'm not buying it. "Is that too young to work here?"

"That's the *perfect* age to work here," I say, inhaling deeply. *Mmmmmm.* She smells delicious. Like cotton candy, and the mouthwatering scent is making me want to taste all of her pink areas to see if they taste as sweet as they smell.

At thirty-three, I'm a bit too old for her by society's standards, but by my standards, she's fresh and ripe and ready to go.

She will be mine.

I'm one of the most powerful CEOs in the state and when I want something I get it. And holy fuck, do I want this girl.

There's just something about her that has me gripped. Fixated. Her smell is rewiring my brain like a computer virus, overriding every thought until all I can think of is her.

I can tell that I'm already obsessed. It didn't take long, but I'm hooked. When she leaves, I'll be pacing around this office like a wild animal, wondering if she's safe, worried that someone is going to steal her from me.

I won't sleep tonight. I won't ever sleep again unless she's beside me where I can keep my protective arms wrapped around her.

She's fidgeting with the arms of the chair as I stare down at her, memorizing every detail of her flawless face. Every inch of her beautiful curves. I want to be able to see her perfectly in my mind when I close my eyes later. I want to picture every detail in one hundred percent accuracy as I jerk off over and over again.

"My mother was supposed to be here," she says, starting to ramble nervously. "But she couldn't make it, so I came instead. I hope that's okay. If you want someone more experienced, my mother can come back tomorrow."

"*No*," I snap, making her jump. "I want *you*."

Her eyes widen and she leans back as I push off the desk and place a hand on each armrest of her chair, trapping her in.

"You're going to be my personal secretary, Bambi" I say, clenching my hands around the armrests. She's so dangerously close. I could just reach out and touch one of those round breasts that have my cock screaming. I could just lean down and take her luscious lips that are waiting to be claimed. "You'll be here every day at eight A.M. You'll do *what* I say, *when* I say. Understood?"

She slowly nods her head up and down, staring at me with large unblinking eyes. Her hands are flat on her thighs and she hasn't moved an inch since I ambushed her, crouching over her chair like I'm going to devour her at any second.

I'm the one trying to trap her here, but I know that *I'm* the one who's really trapped.

My hungry eyes roam down her body, over her huge tits that are moving up and down quickly with her fast breath. Tiny goosebumps appear on her arms as my eyes prowl down to her legs.

"How much experience do you have?" I ask, narrowing my heated eyes on her.

Her tongue darts out of her mouth, quickly licking her lips and the sexy sight makes my hard cock jump in my pants. It's aching with the need to get out and violate her young ripe body.

"Not much," she says in a soft timid voice. "Just some babysitting and I was a lifeguard for two summers."

The thought of her in a bathing suit sitting up on display for every man walking by to see is making my arms flex and my jaw clench. Nobody but me should have the right to look at that body. She's mine now, and no one will ever look at her like that again.

I don't care what I have to do. I don't care how low I have to sink. I'm a powerful guy and I can destroy anyone financially as well as physically. If anyone looks at her again, they'll fucking regret it.

"That's great," I say, biting my bottom lip as I look down at her pussy, wondering if it's wet, wondering what she would do if I just slid my hand up her skirt and touched it. "But that's not what I'm talking about. Are you *experienced?*"

I say the last word slowly as I raise my eyebrow. Her cheeks flush an adorable pink, and I know that she gets what I'm talking about.

I don't care about her ability to take phone calls or sort files. I want to know if any other man has touched her. I want to know if there's a cherry buried deep in there, waiting for me to claim.

"Oh," she says, swallowing hard. She's not breathing anymore as she stares up at me. I'm not breathing anymore either. My heart is racing in anticipation to hear her answer.

I don't know what I'm going to do if she's not a virgin. Fantasies of finding the guy who took what's mine, and making him pay are already racing through my mind.

"No," she whispers, dropping her head. "I haven't..."

The words fall away from her lips, taking all of the stress and anxiety racing through my veins away with it. *Thank fucking God.* I take a deep breath of relief as excitement replaces the worry. She hasn't been touched. I'll be the first man to slide between those sweet thighs and claim her virgin cunt. She'll never want another man after my cock has filled her.

I'll take her without protection and root my seed in her body so she'll be bound to me forever.

"Good," I say as I release the armrests and step back from her. "You're officially hired."

A warm smile spreads across her face, and the sight makes my heart beat so fast it feels like it's going to vibrate out of my chest.

I feel her eyes on me as I walk around the desk and sit in my chair.

Rose is the best secretary in the history of secretaries,

but I don't care about work or my business right now. I would give everything I spent the last two decades working for if it meant spending my days close to Bambi's perfect body. It's all that matters to me now. She's my only priority.

I hit the button on my phone that links me to Rose. "*What can I do for you, Mr. Decker?*" she asks.

"Rose, you know that advanced retirement you wanted?" I ask.

"*Yes?*" her voice is raised. Excited.

"It starts in five minutes."

"*With a full severance package?*" she asks. I can hear her voice trembling.

"Yup," I answer. "And a ten percent bonus."

The phone line goes dead, but I hear a loud squeal through the window.

"What's your name?" I ask Bambi.

"Violet," she says, staring at me in shock. "Violet Martin."

"From now on if someone asks, you tell them your last name is Decker," I demand. One day it will be, and I just want to hear my last name attached to hers.

She tucks a strand of her silky blond hair behind her ear and nods.

"You'll get paid $150,000 for your secretarial and *other* services," I tell her. Her mouth drops open, making my dick ache.

"A hundred and fifty thousand?" she whispers, staring at me in disbelief. I can tell she doesn't have lots of money, and that she doesn't come from much. That will all change today. She won't want for anything for the rest of her life. I'll take care of her every need. Her *every* need.

I cross my arms over my chest as I watch her. "You will

follow my every command," I say, "no matter how uncomfortable it may make you."

She swallows hard, but then nods.

"Come here."

Her body tightens before she reluctantly gets up and walks over, looking at me nervously. I turn my chair as she stops at the side of my desk.

"Come *here*," I command, putting a little more force into my voice.

She hurries over, standing in front of me.

"Let's talk about your dress code."

"Okay," she says in a trembling voice.

My eyes are level with her big tits. I desperately want to rip off her shirt and coat them in my saliva, but I also don't want her running out of here screaming.

"This shirt violates my office dress code," I say, rolling my chair a little closer to her.

She looks down at it as her cheeks redden. "I'm sorry," she says, looking flustered. "I don't have a lot of work clothes, but I'll be—"

"The shirt is fine," I say, licking my lips as I stare at her big tits pressing out against the thin material. It would be better if it was off completely, but that will come later. "It's the buttons that are the problem."

"The buttons?" she asks, looking confused.

She takes in a sharp intake of air as I reach up and slowly undo her top three buttons. My knuckles graze her soft breasts as she watches with excited eyes. "From now on I want you to wear your shirts like this when you're in my office," I say, opening her shirt. *Fuck, she's so perfect*. Her big round tits are barely contained by her bra. They're spilling out over the top and all I can think about is sliding my hard dick between them and then cumming all over her flawless face.

I lean back to take a better look and a low growl rumbles out of my throat when I see her hard nipples showing through her bra. She's liking this. She's turned on as much as I am.

She looks down at her spectacular tits and her cheeks turn pink. "You want me to walk around the building like this?" she asks.

"No," I answer curtly. "This is only for me. When you're in my office and the blinds are closed, this is how you wear your shirt. But I want it buttoned up to the top when you walk around the building. Nobody sees this but me."

Just thinking of her walking around the halls like that where Jason or Mark or any of the other guys in here could drool over her makes my heart rate jack up. These tits are for my eyes alone. I don't even want them to see her curves pressed up against her shirt.

"In fact," I say. "I want you to wear a jacket tomorrow. Do you have a jacket?"

Her blonde hair bounces on her shoulders as she shakes her head. She doesn't look like she has a lot of money for clothes. The shirt she's wearing is old and too small for her, but I fucking love how it looks.

I open a drawer in my desk where I keep some petty cash and grab all of it. I wish I had more on hand to give her, but there's about two grand, which should be enough for some new clothes.

"Take this," I say, slapping the pile of cash on the table. Her eyes widen like crazy when she sees it. "Get some new clothes. Shirts, dresses, skirts, jackets, shoes, but no pants. No panties."

She jerks her head back. "What?"

"No *pants*. No *panties*." My voice is firm. Unmoving. This is not up for negotiation. "Not while you're in *my* office."

She stares at me with her sexy doey eyes as she nods up and down. "Okay, Mr. Decker. Whatever you say."

My lips curl up in a grin. Just the words I wanted to hear.

"I'm glad we're on the same page," I say, slowly looking down at her skirt. "But it seems like you may be in violation of the dress code. Come here, Bambi, and let me check."

She steps toward me immediately. My hands are tingling with the need to explore her young body.

I know this is sexual harassment, but I don't give a fuck. Laws don't matter to me when it comes to her, besides I can tell by her hard nipples, her cute little quickened breaths, and the way her excited eyes keep darting to the outline of my hard cock, that she wants this as much as I do.

I must possess her completely no matter what. No matter what the cost. No matter what the pain and suffering. No matter what laws I have to break.

She will be mine. Every cell in my body will be on fire until she's mine.

I'm having her. No matter what.

She gasps when I touch the warm skin on the outside of her thighs. *Fuck.* If my cock was any harder it would turn to stone. This girl feels even better than I imagined she would.

She's breathing as fast as I am. Her big brown eyes are locked on mine as my hands slide up her legs, and dip under her skirt.

"Shit," she moans under her breath as she takes a small step to the side, slightly parting her legs. Her skirt is raising up in bunches, revealing the soft milky white skin underneath. I lick my lips as her white cotton panties come into view in front of my face. There's a wet spot over her pussy that's slowly getting bigger as I stare at it.

"These are coming off," I say as I slide my palms over the beautiful curve of her ass before gripping the waistband of her panties.

She doesn't say a thing, she just nods up and down quickly as she holds her breath, watching me intently.

I slowly slide her panties down, moaning deeply when her succulent smell hits my nose, making me lightheaded. A blonde tuft of hair comes into view as I peel her panties down, and the thought that I'm the first man to see any of this nearly has me cumming in my pants.

The wet fabric sticks to her pussy lips and only separates when I give it a little tug. I swallow hard as my heart starts hammering in my chest. I'm so close to her virgin cunt that's already so wet and I haven't even touched it yet.

"Your cherry is still in there?" I ask, staring at her swollen pussy as I slide her panties down her legs.

She rests a small hand on my shoulder as she steps out of her panties that are now mine, one foot at a time. "I'm still a virgin," she says in a shy voice. She shouldn't be shy or embarrassed about that. She saved herself for me, which was exactly what she was supposed to do.

"You won't be for long, Bambi," I say, taking her panties and stuffing it into one of the drawers in my desk. She takes her skirt and is about to pull it back down her legs when I snap my head back around.

"Don't," I command. "I'm not done with that yet."

Her big brown eyes are locked on mine as I'm about to tell her what's going to happen next. She's going to sit on the desk in front of me and I'm going to put my mouth on her spread cunt while she plays with her tits. Then I'm going to pull out my raw cock and slide it inside, taking her sweet cherry as I put a baby in her belly.

The lock clicks and the door swings open unexpectedly. Mark walks in. "Mr. Xi is here to sign the—"

"Get the fuck out of here!" I growl.

Bambi quickly slides her skirt down her legs and turns, hiding her open shirt.

Mark's wide startled eyes darts from her to me. I want to take his eyes out for looking at her like this. I want to take his heart out for making her uncomfortable.

"I should go," Bambi says, grabbing the money off the desk before fleeing out of my office like a skittish little fawn. "I'll be back at eight A.M. tomorrow."

I jump up from my chair so fast that it flies back and slams into the wall of windows behind me. "Wait!" I shout, but she disappears past Mark's soon-to-be very bruised face.

"Sorry, boss," he says, suddenly looking very worried as I turn my heated eyes on him. "It's Mr. Xi. Eighty million dollars."

I take a deep breath, trying to calm the fits of rage that are taking over my body.

"Where's Rose?" I snap. "How did you open the door?"

Mark takes a step back, looking around nervously. "Rose is gone. The key was on her desk."

I squeeze my eyes shut and take a deep breath. "I'll be out in a minute. Close the door."

I don't have to ask him twice. He's out of there as fast as humanly possible.

"Fuck," I mutter as I drop down into my chair, rubbing my eyes with my hands. *What the fuck was that?*

One look at the girl and I was completely off-hinged. Completely obsessed.

I let my secretary that I had for the past decade go without a second thought, I nearly a fucked a girl in my office, I brushed off an eighty million dollar client like he was worthless, and my *only* regret was that I didn't handcuff Violet to the bookcase so that she would still be here.

I keep my eyes closed, trying to picture every perfect detail of her face and body as I open the desk drawer and pull out her panties.

"*Fuuuccckkk*," I groan as I stuff them to my nose, smelling her delicious scent while I unbuckle my belt and pull out my thick cock.

It barely takes five strokes of my fist before I bunch them over my dick and cum all over them.

Cumming does nothing to relieve the pressure built up inside. There's a man outside waiting to give me eighty million dollars, and all I can think about is leaving to go find her.

I've never been like this before. I've always been so professional, *always* putting work before women. I haven't had a relationship in years because it took time away from growing my business, and now after ten minutes alone with this girl, I'm ready to throw it all away for a taste of what's waiting between her legs.

I groan as I start jerking off again, desperate to release some of the obsession that's taking root deep in my bones.

What the fuck is happening to me?

I TOLD myself I wasn't going to do this, but deep down, I knew that it was a lie.

I'm watching Violet from my car, looking through her window as she walks around her apartment, making dinner for her mother.

She looks just as beautiful in an old t-shirt and sweat-pants than she did this afternoon. My cock has been rock hard all day, and no matter how many times I jerk off into her panties, it doesn't relieve an ounce of pressure. There's only one thing that will do that, and that is taking her cherry.

Tomorrow. Eight A.M.

I throw my head back and cum in her panties as I picture cumming deep in her warm cunt.

Tomorrow. That cherry will be mine.

3

I CAN'T WIPE THE EXCITED GRIN OFF MY FACE AS THE ROLLS Royce pulls up to the curb in front of *Decker Engineering*. When I walked out of my apartment building this morning there was a beautiful Rolls waiting for me at the curb with a female driver holding a sign that said, *Mrs. Violet Decker*.

I was confused at first, but she handed me a note that explained everything:

You're not to use public transportation anymore. You now have a car service waiting for you twenty-four hours a day, seven days a week. Call 555-679-3076 whenever you need it, but make sure they send you a *female* driver.

I want you in the office no later than 8:00 A.M.

Remember the dress code.

-Mr. Decker

AT FIRST, I wondered how he knew where I lived, but then a grin crept across my lips when I realized where he got my address from. I couldn't help laughing as I pictured Carol on her knees, rummaging through the garbage as she looked for the resume that she crumpled up and threw out.

My pulse starts racing as I look out the car window at the tall building in front of me. It has Mr. Decker's name in big block letters over the door. I get a warm shiver as they look back down at me. Even his name gives me shivers.

I couldn't stop thinking of him last night, and how he had me under his complete control. He didn't tiptoe around what he wanted, or played it subtle. He bossed me around with his perverted demands and it made me so hot that I couldn't do anything but submit to his will.

He should scare me, but he doesn't. We don't know each other at all, but there's a deep connection there—an attraction that gripped my core and rooted itself deep inside me until arousal coursed through my veins, penetrating every nerve in my body.

He did something to me that I still don't understand, but I want more of it. It's all I can think about. My body is craving his touch, yearning for that hard rod that was pushing out against the inside of his pants. I saved my virginity for so long. I just didn't find a guy who I was interested in enough to hand it over to. But all of that changed yesterday. I don't even have to hand it over to Mr. Decker. He's going to *take* it.

"Just call me when you're finished," the driver says, smiling at me as she opens the door. "I'll be here whenever you need me."

I thank her and walk to the building with a spring in my step. It's chilly out in the early morning, but there's heat rushing through my body from my head to my toes as anticipation of what's to come settles in.

I have no idea what to expect today, but I can't wait to find out what Mr. Decker has planned for me.

"You're back," the receptionist says, smiling as I walk in through the door. "And looking good!"

I grin as I glance down at my new outfit. Two thousand dollars bought me enough clothes to throw all of my other old ratty clothes out. I'm wearing a blue and white striped skirt that ends just above my knees with a white blouse and a pink jacket over it just like Mr. Decker requested.

And just like Mr. Decker requested, I'm not wearing any panties underneath. It feels so thrilling to have the cool air blow up and tickle my pussy that's already warm and wet just from stepping into the building.

"I got the job," I say, smiling back at the receptionist. She tells me her name is Ruby and after chatting for a minute I wish her a good day and hurry upstairs. I don't want to keep my mean, demanding boss waiting otherwise he might punish me. On second thought, maybe that would be fun...

Adrenaline rushes through my veins with every floor that the elevator rises. I stare at the button of the top floor as I think back to yesterday for the seven hundredth time since I woke up.

I don't know why I ran.

His hands on me felt so good, and I desperately wanted to see what was going to happen next. But then the door opened and that guy came in, and I just panicked.

I just wasn't prepared for the connection between us to be so strong. I wasn't ready for his hands to take over my body, or for his words to control me so completely. The intense intimacy came out of nowhere. I was putty in his strong hands, and I would have done *whatever* he had ordered me to do.

So when the door opened, I was jerked out of my slutty daze, and I just grabbed the money and ran. Maybe I was scared by the intensity of my attraction to him, maybe I was afraid of the lengths I would have gone to in order to please him, or maybe my fight or flight instinct came in and I just had to run from the big bad alpha beast in front of me. Whatever it was, I spent the rest of the day regretting leaving, and the rest of the night looking forward to this morning.

The elevator opens on the top floor and I take a deep breath before stepping out. It's still early in the morning and there are not too many people in the office yet. The people that have already arrived are busy at work and don't seem to notice me as I walk to Mr. Decker's office.

I'm feeling extremely naked with no underwear on as I walk down the professional-looking halls.

Carol's hardened eyes glare at me as I walk past her office. I just smirk back at her and give her a little wave. *Bitch.*

I retrace my steps from yesterday, walking down the maze of hallways as my heart pounds in my chest. I'm intensely aware of the fact that I have no panties on as I turn the corner and Mr. Decker's large office comes into view. He doesn't seem to be here yet, so I walk to Rose's old desk, which is now mine, and slip into the seat.

I turn on the computer and look around, opening drawers as it loads. My breath catches in my throat when I see my name card on the desk. *Violet Decker. Personal Secretary.*

So, it wasn't just me. He felt it too.

Heavy footsteps echo down the hall and I dart my eyes up just in time to see him walk in. My breath starts to pick up, and my pussy pulses, getting warm and wet with just the sight of him.

He's looking so fuckable in a fitted gray suit, white shirt, and a black tie. His hair is combed to the side again, but it's not as meticulous as yesterday. There are some strands loose, like he's lost a bit of control, and there's a touch of darkness under his eyes, like he couldn't sleep last night.

My heart stops as his eyes connect with mine, sending warm shivers racing through my trembling body.

Holy shit.

I can't breathe. I'm frozen in the chair as he licks his lips while stalking forward. This is what it must feel like to be standing in front of a hungry lion while being wrapped in bacon.

Who knew it would be so arousing?

"Good morning, Mr. Decker," I manage to spit out in a shaky voice. All of the desire and want and need from yesterday comes rushing back with every step that he takes.

He straightens his thin black tie with a tattooed hand as he looks me up and down. "I want you in my office," he says without breaking stride. "*Now.*"

My wet pussy clenches at his demand, and I swear that the suctioning sound is loud enough for him to hear. I jump up from my chair and hurry around the desk as he opens the door and charges into his office.

"Close the door," he orders as he frantically shuts the blinds over the windows.

I do as he says and then lock it, because I have a suspicion of what's about to happen, and I don't want anyone disturbing us like they did yesterday.

He tosses his laptop bag onto the leather couch and undoes the three buttons on the jacket of his suit as he walks behind his desk and sits down.

I can't stop my hands from fidgeting nervously as I stand in front of his desk, awaiting orders.

His dark eyes move up and down my body, making every tiny hair on my skin stand straight up as I stand there awkwardly. He looks so big and powerful sitting behind that desk, so intimidating and sexy with his expensive suit. The whole city of Chicago is visible from the wall of windows all around us. It feels like we're on top of the world.

"I thought I made the dress code clear," he says in a firm voice that's thick with annoyance.

"I'm not wearing any..." I can't say the words. This is my boss and this is all so unprofessional.

My cheeks burn as his hard eyes fall to my chest.

"Jacket off," he demands.

I quickly unbutton the jacket and slide it off my arms. He nods in approval as I toss it over the back of the chair in front of his desk.

"Now the buttons."

My muscles are twitching with nerves, but my pussy is clenching in excitement as I unbutton the top three buttons and open my shirt. I'm wearing a new white lacy bra that finally fits for once, and I'm secretly happy that he seems to like it.

His eyes never leave my chest as he takes a deep ragged breath. My nipples are painfully hard as he stares at me with a hungry look.

"Your panties?" he asks, rubbing his chin as he watches me with piercing eyes.

I shake my head. "I'm not wearing any."

"Come here," he commands. "The boss needs to check."

I'm intensely aware of my pounding heartbeat as I walk toward him with my mouth watering. He turns his chair as I come around his desk and stand in front of him.

"Lift up your skirt and show me your cunt," he demands. I swallow hard as I watch his unmoving face. He's totally serious, and although every rational thought in my head should be screaming at me to leave, the only thoughts I can hear are from my aching pussy that's begging to be shown.

I take a deep breath and grab the hem of my skirt, and slowly pull it up my thighs. His eyes widen with every inch that it rises, and I can't help but feel sexy as hell that I'm turning this big powerful man on.

He lets out a low groan when I lift my new skirt up over my pussy, showing him that I'm ready to obey his every command. He licks his lips as he stares between my legs, and my body reacts in a strong way. Every thought in my head is a craving for him to touch it. I want him to slide his fingers into it. I want him to taste it, smell it, and finally to thrust his big cock into it, and make it his forever.

He clears his throat and nods, never taking his eyes off of my throbbing sex. "Good job, Bambi," he says in a low throaty voice. "You can let it go now."

I let go of my skirt, and it falls back down to my knees. I just stand there with a sense of loss as I wait for him to tell me what to do next.

"We have a *long* day full of *hard* work," he says, straightening up in his chair. "Are you ready for it?"

I lick my lips as I quickly glance down at the hard bulge in his pants. "Yes," I say with a nod. I've never been more ready.

"Good," he says, taking a deep breath as he looks up at

me with lust in his dark eyes. "You're my new secretary and I have to test how well you follow orders."

I gulp as his hands move to his belt buckle.

"Now get on your knees and suck my cock."

My mouth waters at hearing the dirty words come from his mouth. I can't think properly. My brain is a jumble of incoherent thoughts and desires, all focused on Mr. Decker's hard cock. Before I can stop myself, I'm kneeling in front of him—the rough carpet scratching my knees—and sliding his leather belt through the buckle.

His hard cock looks so long, traveling along the inside of his thigh. I lick my lips as I hurry to get it free.

"I need to know that you're going to follow my *every* command," he says as my excited fingers reach for the button of his pants. "Part of your job, the most *important* part, is doing what I say, when I say it. Do you think you can handle that, Bambi?"

I nod up and down as I pull his zipper down. "I'll do *whatever* you say."

His deep dominant words always put me in a trance, and I couldn't resist him even if I wanted to.

"Good," he says, grinning as he watches me tug his pants down his hips. "Because I haven't been able to stop thinking about your big round tits, and your wet little pussy all night. My dick has been aching for some release, and your hot little mouth is going to provide it for me. Understand?"

I can't answer. I can barely breathe, let alone talk, so I just let my hands do the talking. I pull his tight boxer briefs down and gasp as his long hard cock juts out in front of my face.

It's beautiful. Thick, strong, and as dominant as him. All I can think about is how good it will feel when it dominates my body, stretching and filling me completely.

I've never touched a cock before, but my lack of experience is made up by my enthusiasm. I grab it in a firm grip and lick up the thick underside from the base to the top. Delicious white beads of pre-cum appear out of the tiny hole in the head, and I'm licking up each drop and moaning as Mr. Decker loosens his tie and watches with approval.

"That's good," he groans as I open up wide, and take him in—wrapping my lips around his thick shaft.

My pussy is dripping wet as I swirl my tongue around him, loving the salty sweet taste of his cum. It's making me so wet that my thighs are sticky.

"Mmmmm," I moan as I take him even deeper into my mouth, hammering his shaft with my hand as I suck his big cock.

He yanks off his tie and tosses it onto his desk as I coat every inch of his dick with my hungry tongue. I thought blowjobs were supposed to feel good for the guy, but this feels *so fucking good* that I can't imagine it feels better for him than it does for me.

He undoes the top two buttons of his shirt as I suck him harder, and then sinks his strong powerful hands into my hair. My pussy is on fire as he grabs my head and guides my mouth up and down his cock wherever he wants my lips to go.

"You should have put this talent on your resume, Bambi," he says between heavy breaths. "You're going to get employee of the fucking century for the way you're sucking my cock."

He starts breathing a little heavier and groaning a little louder as I slide my tight lips up and down him a little faster.

"How do you like your boss' big cock in your slutty little

mouth, Bambi?" he asks as his grip tightens on my head. I *fucking love it*. I would do this for free, all day, every day.

I hope there's not a day that goes by without his cock in my mouth.

The fact that people are walking around outside in the halls, obliviously walking from office to office with their morning coffee while I'm servicing the boss in the best possible way is making it even hotter. It feels so dirty and slutty, and I absolutely *love* it.

"All right, Bambi," he gasps as his massive chest rises and falls above me. "I'm going to cum in that sexy little mouth of yours, and you're going to be a good little secretary and drink it all down. *Every* drop of my cum."

I pick up the pace, working him hard with my lips and tongue, desperately wanting to feel his warm cum coating my mouth. I want to drink it up. I want a part of him inside me so when I'm in my lonely bed tonight I can know that he's still with me.

"*Fuck*," he groans, squeezing his eyes closed as his arms and chest flex. I open my throat and take him in as deep as I can, waiting for it.

His huge cock pulses against my tongue and then several long warm streams of cum fill my mouth, making us both moan so loud that the people outside can probably hear.

Not like I care. Satisfying my boss is the only thing that matters now.

I swallow down every last drop of his hot cum and moan as I suck on his swollen head, trying to tease out any last reluctant drops.

Mr. Decker holds my head and tilts it up until my eyes are looking into his. His cock is still in my mouth and I'm slowly moving my lips up and down it in case any late drops of cum drip out.

"Well done, Bambi," he says with a satisfied nod. "But we're not done yet."

My wet pussy clenches as I wonder what's next.

"Take off all your clothes and bend over my desk," he says in a firm voice. "It's time to get a taste of what I'm paying for."

4

MR. DECKER

MY COCK IS STILL ROCK HARD EVEN THOUGH MY HOT NEW secretary just sucked out every last drop of cum inside. I lean back and watch as she wipes the corner of her lips with her finger, stands up, and starts taking off her clothes.

I'm stroking my cock as I watch her. The light from the rising sun is shining through the floor-to-ceiling windows, lighting up her young supple body in exquisite detail.

Her shirt is the first thing to come off, and I shake my head in disbelief as I stare at her tits. How could one girl be so sexy? She's the hottest thing I've ever seen. I would have paid her a million dollars a year if she'd have asked me.

My chest tightens as she unhooks her bra. She glances at the locked door quickly before sliding her lacy white bra down her arms and letting it fall to the floor.

She keeps her hands cupping her breasts and covering her nipples like a little tease, but one word of warning from me has her letting them go.

"*Bambi*," I warn. She releases her huge tits, and I groan as they bounce down her chest. Her nipples are hard and pointing in the air, waiting for me to suck on.

I can't resist. She lets out a scared little whimper as I lunge forward and grab her hips in my hands, gripping her tightly as I pull her to me. Her tits jiggle as they bounce forward, her perfect pink nipples crashing into my lips. I take one in my mouth, sucking as much of it as I can while I cup her other tit in my hand, massaging it while my dick starts aching once again.

Her whimpers turn to moans as I swirl my tongue around her nipple, making it even harder. She buries her hands in my hair, pulling me closer as she arches her back. I take my time with each breast, licking, teasing, sucking, nibbling, and caressing every inch of them.

When I finally pull away, she's breathing as heavily as I am.

"Skirt. Off." I'm barking orders like a damn caveman, but I can't help it with this girl. All I can think about is getting to that young virgin pussy and breeding her. I want my sperm swimming to her waiting womb as quickly as possible. I want her to be carrying my child. I want her dependent on me. I never want her to leave.

Even I think this need to control her—to *own* her—is fucked up, but it's taking over my mind and body. I can't fight it anymore. I don't want to fight it anymore. I just want her to be mine, and I'll do whatever it takes to make that happen.

Her big tits jiggle as she wiggles out of her skirt. *Fuck, this view is incredible.* I'm paying for the company to be on the top floor of the building so we can have this ridiculously good view of the Chicago cityscape, but I'll never even so much as glance at it again while this beauty is in my office.

I'm stroking my hard cock again as her new skirt slides down her thighs, revealing the lush tuft of blonde pubic hair that had me tossing and turning all night. Her smell of desire hits my nose and my head drops back on the chair as I jerk myself off even harder.

The skirt tumbles to the floor and bunches up around her ankles. I take a deep breath, feeling like I've just run a marathon as she steps out of the skirt and stands in front of me completely naked.

My eyes dart to her pussy, which is already glistening in the early morning sunlight.

"I bet if I touch you there, you'd already be soaking wet for me," I say, staring at it. "Isn't that right, Bambi?"

She licks her lips and grins. "Only one way to find out."

Fuck, I love this girl. She steps her left foot to the side, opening her legs for me as I release my cock and lean forward.

She lets out a little gasp as I place a meaty palm on the inside of her thigh and slowly drag it up. Her skin is so soft. Untouched. Unspoiled. I'm the first man to see this, to feel this, and that is making this so much sweeter.

My hand finally reaches her soft pussy lips and her whole body shudders when I touch her there. Her eyes close and she lets out a low moan as I glide my fingers through her soaking wet folds.

"You're even wetter than I thought," I say with a grin. "You like sucking your boss' cock?"

"I fucking love it," she answers in a throaty groan. "Your cock is so big."

"It's going to feel even bigger when I slide it inside here," I say as I glide my finger through her folds and trace it around the tight little opening. Her hole is so tiny. It's so fucking tight that it clamps around the tip of my finger, squeezing it. "Oh fuck, Bambi, that's tight. I can't wait to see what it feels like around my cock."

I don't need to feel a hymen to know that this pussy still has its cherry. It's virgin tight.

Her mouth drops open and a little whimper falls from her lips when I find her clit and rub it in small circles.

"You ever touch yourself down here?" I ask, smiling as I watch the intense pleasure on her face.

She shakes her head, making her blonde hair bounce around on her bare shoulders. "Never," she gasps. "You're the first to do anything like this."

"You like it when I do this?" I ask, already knowing the answer.

"*Yes*," she gasps as her body convulses. "It's *so* fucking good."

"This is just the start of what I'm going to do to you," I say, sliding my hand back out.

"No," she gasps, looking down at me in a panic now that I'm not touching her anymore. Her brown eyes are glossy and clouded with lust. She's breathing heavily as she looks at my fingers that are coated in her sticky juices.

"See how wet you are?" I ask, showing her my fingers. Her eyes widen as I bring them to my mouth and suck on them, drinking down every last drop of her honey. It tastes like sweet innocence.

"Turn around," I command. "Bend over the desk."

One taste and my body is screaming for more. She steps between me and the desk, showing me her perfect ass. My hands are already on it as she bends over the desk, pressing her big round tits on my open agenda. That's perfect because my agenda just got cleared. Her naked body is the only thing on it now.

I spread her ass cheeks and groan as I stare at her pussy from behind. It's so pink and untouched and fucking beautiful. Brand new and in mint condition. But it won't be for long.

I lick my lips as I dip my head forward.

"Oh, shit," she moans as I drag my tongue up her wet cunt, lapping up her warm sugary nectar. It tastes so sweet and as I dip my tongue into the little crease in the middle, it tastes even sweeter.

Her hips start to move, grinding against my mouth as I squeeze her ass cheeks and bury my tongue in deeper. Her back is arched and she's filling the office with moans as she gives me her pussy juice. I greedily take every drop as I stare at her pink asshole in front of me.

When my lips wrap around her clit she cums, and a rush of warm delicious juices coats my mouth. I'm in heaven right now with my tongue lodged deep in her cunt, and by the way she's whipping her head from side to side as her legs shake—she looks like she's right there on the cloud next to me.

"*Oh*, Mr. Decker," she moans, loving how I'm moving my mouth on her.

I still haven't told her my name. I like it better when she calls me Mr. Decker.

She starts moaning louder and louder as I bring her to another orgasm. She gasps as I press my thumb onto her pink asshole, applying a bit of pressure as she cums on my mouth.

My cock is so hard. It's begging me to take her virginity, and after I make her cum one more time, I stand up, about to give him what he's screaming for.

Her head whips back as my lips and tongue disappear from her hot swollen cunt. She looks up at me with glazed over eyes and an open mouth. Her back is moving up and down with quick ragged breaths as she thrusts her ass in the air, hoping to goad my lips back to her sweetness.

I fight the urge to make her cum for a fourth time with my tongue, and stand up instead.

I'm still fully dressed with only my cock sticking out. I take out my cufflinks and roll my sleeves up my thick fore-arms as I watch her moan on the desk and wiggle her pussy in the air like she's desperate for me to fill it.

"Are you ready to please your boss?" I ask, grinning as I loosen my tie.

She nods her head up and down, too far gone to form coherent sentences.

"You got my balls so full of cum that they're aching," I say as I grip my cock and step up to her. She moans deeply as I slap her ass cheek with my cock and drag it over her supple curves. Her skin is the softest I've ever felt, and it still feels like sandpaper compared to the softness of her pussy.

"My cock is ready to take you, Bambi," I say as I slide the head through her silky folds, making her gasp. "It's already dripping with cum. Are you going to take every drop that I give you?"

She nods her head up and down as she bites her bottom lip and moans.

"My cock is going in raw," I warn her. "No protection. Nothing to stop you from getting pregnant. I'm going in bare and you'll be as good as bred once I slide this long dick inside you. I need you in my life for good, Bambi, and once I get inside that sweet cunt you'll be bound to me forever. You understand?"

She looks back at me with her big brown eyes and my heart hurts from her beauty. "I understand," she moans through parted lips. "I want it. Everything you just said."

"That's *my* girl," I say as I squeeze an ass cheek with one hand and drag my cock over her cute little asshole with the other. "You've been mine since the moment I saw you walk past the conference room, but after this, you'll be mine in every sense of the word. You'll be bound to me like we're wearing handcuffs. I'm going to keep you forever."

"That's what I want," she moans as she thrusts her ass in the air, desperately trying to tease me into taking her pussy. "I want to be *yours*."

She was going to be mine regardless of her answer. There was no way I was going to let this pussy go without claiming it.

My Bambi will be in good hands. I'll make damn sure that she's always taken care of, but in exchange, I want her like this every day: legs open, ass in the air, and ready for me the second my cock gets hard.

She grips the opposite side of the desk as I press the thick head of my cock into her tight opening. "Good idea, Bambi," I say, grinning as her knuckles turn white. "Hold on tight because I'm gonna fuck you hard."

She throws her head back and lets out a whimper as I give her what she was begging for. I push my hard cock into her tight little hole, clenching my teeth as I feel it squeeze my dick with so much pressure that it makes my chest flex.

"Oh fuck, Bambi," I growl as I push in a little deeper. Her cherry is coming next and I don't want the whole fucking floor to hear her cries so I cover her mouth with my hand. "This might hurt a bit, my love," I warn as I muffle the sound of her whimpers with my hand. "Soon it will only feel like heaven whenever you take my cock, but this time it might hurt."

I look down at her puckered asshole and then thrust in hard, breaking through her virgin barrier. She cries out into my hand and although I tried to muffle the sound, the people outside surely heard that. But I don't fucking care. What are they going to do? It's a perk of being the boss.

"You okay, Bambi?" I ask as her virgin walls close around me. She nods her head up and down as I slide my dick all the way in, pressing my hard pelvis against her soft ass.

"Better than good," she moans. I release her mouth for now, gripping her hips instead as I slide back out and get ready for another thrust. My dick is coated in her virginity and the sight nearly makes me cum on the spot. I could if I let go, but I want this moment to last, so I clench my jaw and push through the feeling.

"Fuck, your cunt is so tight," I grunt as I slide back inside, enjoying the squeeze of every inch. After a few thrusts, her pussy starts to loosen up a bit and I can move a little faster.

"It feels so fucking good," she moans, rocking her ass back to meet me with every thrust. "I wasn't expecting *this*."

"It feels like that because you're *mine*," I say, hitting her with strong pumps of my hips. "Your pussy was made for my cock. My dick hits every curve, every spot. It was designed for your cunt, Bambi. And it will be in here every day until you take your last breath."

"That sounds fucking *perfect*," she moans as she drops her head onto the table, pressing her forehead against the smooth wood.

I start giving her harder, longer, deeper strokes, pumping my hips at a ruthless pace. The heavy oak desk squeaks as it skids across the floor with every powerful thrust.

Her whimpers turn into cries, which get louder and louder the harder I fuck her. She starts screaming so loud that the whole floor must know what's happening behind this closed door, but I don't give a shit. I'm not shutting her up. I'm not taking any of her pleasure away. I'm king of this office and Bambi is my queen. She can do whatever the fuck she wants.

My employees will just have to get used to it because I'm going to be fucking my hot new secretary multiple times a day in here from now on. If they don't like it, they can leave.

I grab a fistful of her blonde hair and give it a little tug as I fuck her from behind, slamming the front of my muscular thighs into hers. They smack with every stroke and the smacking gets louder as I feel an orgasm rushing forward.

"Fuck, Bambi," I grunt through gritted teeth. "You ready for my hot cum?"

I squeeze her hair in my fist even tighter as she lets out a loud cry. "*Yes!*" she moans. "Cum in my pussy. Make me *yours!*"

My whole body is flexed as I squeeze her hips and thrust in hard, rooting my cock deep inside her as close to her virgin womb as possible. With a deep roar, I empty my cum in her body and pray that my sperm finds her ripe womb and claims it.

Her body tenses up as I drop my load, and I feel her pussy pulsing all around me as she cums on my cock. Her knuckles turn white as she grips the desk and screams out my name. "Oh, Mr. Decker," she shouts, *way* too loud as her body trembles.

Let everybody hear. I don't care. They'll know that this pussy is mine and she is off limits. The guys will know to keep their eyes on their shoes when she's in the room, and the women won't treat her in the cold way that some older women treat young pretty girls.

After our orgasms have dissipated, I pull out of her and turn her around on the desk so she's lying on her back with her legs resting on my shoulders.

She's looking so sexy with her big tits in the air—her nipples flattened from being pushed so hard into the desk. Her blonde hair is spread on the desk around her like a halo as she looks up at me with her big sexy Bambi eyes.

"Fuck," she says, licking her lips as she rubs her forehead. "I wasn't expecting it to feel *that* good."

My cock is resting on her swollen pussy and it's getting hard again with the gorgeous view of her lying naked in front of me.

I slide it back inside her warm wetness and gently rub her clit as I give her slow gentle thrusts.

"Best secretary ever," I say with a grin as my cock hardens fully inside of her. She feels so damn good. I don't know if I'll ever be able to stop fucking her.

She giggles, but they quickly turn into moans as I pick up the pace, fucking her again with the same urgency as before. I grab the front of her thighs and pull her body into mine with every thrust, biting my bottom lip as I watch her round tits bouncing up and down.

It's not long before we're both cumming again, and I fall into her waiting arms as I empty my seed inside her.

She holds me tightly as the phone rings beside us, jerking us out of the heavenly moment.

I'm about to reach for it to launch it across the room when she stops me. "I am your secretary too," she says with a grin as she picks up the phone. "Mr. Decker's office. How can I help you?"

I stare at her pink lips as someone speaks to her on the other line.

"I'll let him know," she says in a professional voice. "Thank you."

She hangs up the phone and I kiss her mouth, sliding

my tongue over hers before she can say who that was and ruin the moment with business talk.

"Mmmmm," she moans as I taste every inch of her mouth. This girl is perfect. I'm going to spend the rest of my life loving her and taking care of her every need.

"That was Mr. Xi," she says when we pull away. "He's waiting for you in the conference room. Something about finalizing the deal?"

I take a deep breath and stand up, climbing off her. I want to stay here with her all day, but there's eighty million dollars in my pocket if I run out to sign the contract.

"Stay here," I say as I pull my boxer briefs up and over my cock. It's still coated in her juices, just the way I like it.

Violet gets up and bends over to grab her clothes off the ground. *Fuck.* Her ass is perfect. Who the hell would mind coming to work every day if this was waiting for you?

"I might be a while," I say, watching her tits as she gets dressed. "This guy likes to drag out the signing process. It might take a few hours."

She slides her bra on as I straighten my tie. "Hurry back," she says, stepping on her toes and giving me a kiss on the lips. "I'm one of the only few employees in the world who likes to have their boss around."

"I wonder why," I say as I drag my hand over her pussy, cupping it like it belongs to me. Because it does.

She giggles as she pushes away from my grasp, putting the rest of her clothes on.

I can already picture her with a round belly, my child growing inside. A rush of warm contentment flows through me at the thought. I can't wait to see that.

"Cancel all of my appointments for the week," I say as I roll my sleeves back down my tattooed forearms, watching her bare pussy as she wiggles into her dress. "I'm going to be busy. *Very* busy."

She grins as her eyes light up. "I like the sound of that."

"Use my phone," I say. "Your cheeks are still red from all those orgasms, and that's for me alone to see."

"*Whatever* you say, Mr. Decker." She sits down in my chair and lifts her feet on my desk, watching me with a grin on her sexy lips. She only has her skirt and bra on, and the view of her sitting at my desk is making me want to tell Mr. Xi to take his eighty million dollars and go take a hike.

I grin as I step up to her and grab her ankles in a strong grip. I pull them apart and lick my lips as I look down at her spread pussy under her skirt. It looks irresistible.

My cock starts to harden again and I grab my belt buckle.

Mr. Xi can wait.

5

MR. DECKER

IT'S AFTER NINE O'CLOCK AT NIGHT BY THE TIME MR. XI SIGNS the fucking contract. I have never been more annoyed in my life to get eighty million dollars.

The office is empty when I finally get out of the conference room. The janitor is walking around with a vacuum cleaner, cleaning the carpets.

"Don't clean my desk," I tell him. Violet's virginity and pussy juices are still on it and I want to keep it like that for a little while longer.

I had told her to go home a few hours ago when it was clear that Mr. Xi wasn't going to sign anytime soon. He's paying us to build him a trio of towers in Shanghai, which will be the tallest structures in the Chinese city, and he wanted to go through every excruciating detail with me. After a few hours, he finally signed and transferred the money over.

I couldn't get out of there fast enough. I should be heading out to celebrate, but all I can think of is climbing onto my Bambi and burying my cock into her once again.

I don't like the thought of her being out in the world

without me, but the car service that I ordered for her helps take some of my fears away. There is no way I would let her go back on public transportation where anyone could just touch her or leer at what's mine alone to look at. She'll have a female driver from now on.

After showing Mr. Xi out, I grab my things and hurry down to the parking lot. I jump in my Mercedes and fly out of the indoor parking lot with one thing on my mind.

I'm at Violet's apartment building in record time. My cock hardens just from knowing she's near.

This building is falling apart and is located in a bad part of town. I don't want my greatest treasure in the world living in a place like this. She deserves the best in the world, and I'm determined to give it to her.

There's a creepy looking guy hanging out in front of the door, smoking a cigarette. The thought of my innocent Bambi having to walk by guys like that on her way home has my chest tightening and my heart pounding.

I'm throwing the car in park when the front door opens and Violet walks out holding a garbage bag. The guy is immediately by her side, saying something to her as she cringes. She hurries to the garbage bin, and he keeps the same pace, saying something about how she owes him rent and that she can come to his room and pay him with her other assets.

I don't even take the time to roll up my windows or pull out my car keys. There's a vicious pounding in my ears as adrenaline rages through my body.

"Hey!" I scream in a savage roar as I charge at him with my hands squeezed into fists. He turns to me in shock as I crash into him, grabbing his sweater in my hands and lifting him off his feet. His cigarette goes flying as I smash him into the huge metal garbage bin, shaking it to its core as I bash his head into it.

"That's *my* girl!" I snarl into his face, feeling all of the possessiveness that I have for this girl overflow out of me like an erupting volcano. "She's fucking *mine* and any guy who tries to get that honey is going to have to answer to *me*."

I ram him back into the metal bin even harder this time. His eyes are rolling back in his head as he looks up at me with panic. He collapses into a heap as I drop him on the wet cement.

Violet is still holding the garbage bag in her hands, staring at me in shock.

"Did he touch you?" I snarl, sounding like a wild animal.

She shakes her head.

"Did he try to?"

She nods, and my body goes rigid with the need to open his skull. I turn to him, taking heavy violent breaths as I watch him cower at my feet. He tried to soil my property. He tried to take her innocence for his own.

He's going to fucking pay for that.

"She owed me rent," he says, lifting his hands up to protect his face. He's going to need a lot more than shaky hands to protect himself from me. "I was just trying to collect."

"You were trying to *collect* all right," I say as I grab his sweater and yank him back up. "Now it's my turn to *collect*. How much does she owe you?"

His voice is shaky. He looks terrified. "Three months rent. Twelve hundred dollars."

I reach into my pocket and grab a wad of cash. There should be at least enough there to cover the rent and some of the stitches I'm about to give him. I stuff it in his pocket with one hand as my other one clenches around his arm.

"This is for the rent." His eyes widen as I cock my fist back. "And this is for trying to take my girl's innocence."

Violet turns away as I slam my fists into his body over and over again, one for every dirty thought he had of her. I'd kill him if she wasn't here watching, but I don't want her seeing any more than this.

He falls to the ground unconscious and I give him one last kick before leaving him by the garbage where he belongs.

"Get your things," I say as I walk up to her. "You're living with me now."

She just swallows as she nods up and down. "But my mother," she says, looking up at the building. "I can't leave her here."

"Your mother will be taken care of," I say, pulling out my cell phone. "I own a bunch of condos around town that I rent out. I have a beautiful two bedroom overlooking the water in Lincoln Park that she can have."

"Have?" Violet repeats, dropping her mouth in shock.

"It's all hers," I say. And I mean it. I'll have the deed transferred to her name first thing tomorrow morning. "Anyone who creates something as perfect as you deserves a nice place to live."

She runs into my arms and hugs me. "Thank you," she says, kissing my lips. "We've never had anything before. You've given me so much already."

"It's just the start, Bambi," I say, kissing the top of her head. "You and your mother won't be denied a thing. I have a job for her if she wants to work, or I'll pay her bills and give her money if she wants to retire."

My sweet little fawn hugs me again, and my heart melts with how good it feels.

"Go tell your mom that she has a new fully furnished

penthouse condo waiting for her," I say, tapping her ass. "I'll have someone collect her things tomorrow and bring them to her."

"She's going to be so happy," she says, clasping her hands together and squealing in delight.

This girl is going to move in with me and have my child.

I'm so happy too.

~

"I CAN'T BELIEVE the size of this thing," she says, spreading her arms wide as she spins around her huge walk-in closet. I knew this moment was coming eventually so I made a couple of calls today and had my personal shopper fill it with brand new clothes in her size. She has everything she could possibly need and more.

"There are so many shoes," she says, her eyes lighting up as she looks up at them on the rows and rows of shelves. "I can't believe you did this. No one has ever done anything like this for me before."

I grin as I see the smile on her face. I would do anything for that smile.

She bounces around my penthouse condo oohing and ahhing at everything. "This is all yours now," I say as I follow her from room to room. "It's your home as much as mine."

"I can't believe it," she says, her eyes widening as she walks into the huge bathroom. "I was about to sleep on the street, and now I'm living like a princess."

"You're my princess," I say, stepping up behind her and sliding my arms around her body. She sighs contently as I glide my palm down her stomach and slide my fingers into her jeans.

"Mmmmmm," she moans as I find her clit and rub it gently. She's already so wet for me. "Let's try out this huge shower," she says as she reaches back and runs her palm along my hard cock, making me groan.

I get her naked in record time and she turns on the shower and steps in while I take off my suit. She's so perfect, and I can't believe she's mine.

I'm definitely going to marry this one. I want her bound to me in as many ways as possible. Legally. Physically. Spiritually. I want it all.

The water is warm but her body is warmer. I grab under her thighs and pick her up easily, holding her against the wall as I slide my hard cock into her warm wetness.

"Oh, Bambi," I moan as she digs her face into the nook of my neck. She holds me tightly as I start thrusting in deep. The water is pouring over us as our bodies meld as one.

"I still don't know your name," she moans. Her hard nipples are pressing into my thumping chest. "Are you ever going to tell me or do I have to call you Mr. Decker for the rest of my life?"

I grin as I fuck her harder, shutting that pretty little mouth up by turning her words into deep moans.

"You can call me sir, boss, Mr. Decker, or Mr. CEO," I answer as I drive in deep, hitting her with faster strokes. Her body starts to shake as I draw an orgasm out of her.

"Okay," she gasps as her pussy clenches on my cock and she cums. "Fuck, Mr. CEOoooooo."

6

VIOLET

Six months later

"KEEP YOUR FUCKING EYES OFF HER!" my new fiancee warns.

"I don't think he speaks English," I say, trying to hold back my giggle as the Chinese construction worker runs away.

"He understood *that*," Derek says, stepping up beside me and sliding a protective hand over my belly. I'm six months pregnant and he loves my baby bump. I'm glad that he does because I'm hornier than ever and can't get enough of his hard cock.

Derek proposed to me—yes I finally learned that his name was Derek, but I still like to call him Mr. Decker—about two weeks after my job interview. I had been living with him for over a week and I already knew that I would never want anyone else. I had known since the first time he burst into Carol's office and grabbed me like a horny barbarian.

We got married the next day, and I've been in heaven ever since.

"It's coming along great," Derek says, looking down at the cement foundation of one of the three tower complexes that Mr. Xi ordered. We're in Shanghai to see how the progress is coming along. "I couldn't have done it without you, Bambi," he says, kissing my temple.

"I don't know about that," I say, smiling at the compliment. I quickly got the swing of things around the office, and when my perverted boss isn't pulling my clothes off and bending me over his desk, I'm a really big help. I managed to get the Chinese consulate to give us the construction permits right away when there's usually a year-long wait. Mr. Decker gave me a bonus for pulling that one off. It was long and hard, and I loved every inch of it.

Mr. Xi comes over and thanks us for all of the good work we've done. He's very pleased with the tower designs and is considering ordering two more.

"Mr. Decker, your sexy secretary would like her own tower," I say, grinning up at him after Mr. Xi leaves us.

"I'll build you a high one and lock you at the top to make sure you'll never leave me," he says, holding me close.

I slide my hand down past his hard abs and he groans when I feel his cock harden under my touch. "That's not the kind of tower I want."

His breathing picks up as he looks around. There's a nice hotel across the street and he points to it. "I'll go tell Mr. Xi that we're leaving. Go book us a room."

I grin as I pull a key out of my pocket and hold it up. "Already did." We never get through the day without wanting to tear each other's clothes off so I always plan for the inevitable. I snuck over to the hotel when he was busy, and rented a room, knowing this moment would come.

He grabs the key and crushes his lips to mine.

"Best. Secretary. Ever."

I moan as he kisses me deep, making my pussy pulse.

Best. Boss. Ever.

EPILOGUE

VIOLET

Six years later

"SPECIAL DELIVERY FOR MR. DECKER," I say in a sexy voice as I lean against the door frame of my husband's office.

His face breaks out into a grin as he looks up from his computer and sees me. "Fuck, you're beautiful," he says, shaking his head as he looks me up and down.

"You say that every time."

"I *think* that every time," he says, licking his lips as he adjusts his tie.

Six years and three children later and he still thinks I'm the most beautiful woman in the world. I'm sure that he's going to think I'm just as beautiful after my fourth.

"That round belly makes me so hard," he says, standing up so fast that his chair bumps into the wall of windows behind him. "Lock the door."

I giggle mischievously as I close the door and lock it.

Derek is darting around the office, closing the blinds to give us some privacy for what's about to come.

I'm seven months pregnant with our fourth child and haven't visited him in his office for a while. He doesn't want me working when I'm pregnant, so I've been off for the past few months. He wants me safe at home, and I don't mind a bit. How can I complain when we have a beautiful condo overlooking the city? Besides, I've been so tired making a human that I don't mind resting at home.

"God, I miss having you here," he says, taking a deep breath as he watches me walk to his desk. I sit down in his chair and grin when I look out the window at his new secretary.

"Is John not cutting it for you?" I ask with a chuckle.

Derek closes the blinds, shutting my view of the back of John's head. I made him get a male secretary when I took a leave of absence for my pregnancy. He's not the only one who's a little obsessive and jealous.

"Not nearly as good as you," he says, walking over with his rock hard dick totally visible in his fitted designer pants.

"I'm sorry, Derek," I say.

He crosses his arms over his massive chest and narrows his heated eyes on me, making me gulp. "What did you call me?"

"Mr. Decker," I say, quickly correcting myself. I'm going to pay for that.

My pussy gets soaking wet as I watch him take off his cufflinks and roll his shirt up his thick tattooed forearms. He's as sexy as ever, and I still can't believe that he's obsessed with me.

"Did you already forget the rules of my office?" he asks, taking deep heavy breaths as he walks forward.

I bite my bottom lip as I shake my head.

"Prove it," he says, licking his lips. "Show me your cunt."

A flood of warmth flows through me as I stand up for him and pull up my dress. He lets out a low groan of approval when he sees that I'm not wearing any panties.

He pulls out his hard cock and hits the button on the phone that connects him to John. "Cancel all of my appointments for the afternoon," he says, grinning at me with lust in his eyes. "I'm going to be busy for a *long* time."

A shiver ripples through me as he takes his finger off of the phone and turns back to me with his hard cock in his hand.

"Dress off. Mouth open. On your knees."

He's as demanding as ever, but there's nothing I love more than obeying his every command.

I wouldn't change a thing of my Mr. CEOoooooo.

The End!

DON'T BE SHY. COME FOLLOW ME...

I WON'T BITE UNLESS YOU ASK ME TO

 facebook.com/OliviaTTurnerAuthor

 instagram.com/authoroliviatturner

 goodreads.com/OliviaTTurner

 amazon.com/author/oliviatturner

 bookbub.com/authors/olivia-t-turner

THE VIRGIN AUCTION

BY OLIVIA T. TURNER

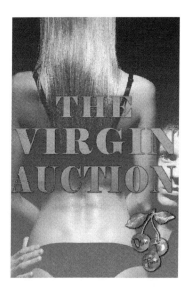

These Billionaires want to pay for my cherry but he's
going to *take it* for free.

I desperately needed the money.

My virginity was the only thing I had left to sell.

But when an Over The Top billionaire gets his hands on me,

I no longer care about money...

Max can give me more than money.

He can give me feelings that I never knew were possible.

He can give me his protection.

He can give me a baby.

Only thing is, I'm never allowed to leave...

Get it on Amazon!

CHAPTER ONE OF THE VIRGIN AUCTION

Max

"WHAT THE FUCK DID I GET MYSELF INTO?"

I shake my head as I sink into the large comfy leather chair and take a sip of the smooth scotch they provided. The lights dim inside my little room as the lights flick on behind the dark glass.

The auction is starting.

I'm going to kill my assistant. This was Jeff's idea. He's always going on and on about how I need to find a good woman in my life.

"It will settle you down," he always says. "You should find a girl who can help dull some of that edge you've got going on."

I like my edge. I'm as sharp as a Samurai sword and in the world of billionaires, you have to be sharp.

Maybe Jeff has a point but fuck, a virgin auction? Who would dream up something so twisted?

A door opens and the first girl walks out onto the stage. It's set up like an octagon. Each side is a private booth with a virgin-loving billionaire behind it. The walls are made up of one-way glass so nobody can see who is behind it. It's total privacy for everyone except for the timid girl who's walking under the bright lights in the middle of it all. She's wearing baby doll pajamas with her blonde hair done up in curls with a nice big pink bow on top.

There's a screen at my feet with the girl's name and stats:

Sarah Matthews.

Nineteen.

Virgin.

5'6. 119 lbs.

This is so twisted. The screen lights up as someone makes a bid. The bids go up in $25,000 increments. I look down at the green button on my armrest and shake my head. These creeps aren't getting any of my hard earned cash. I don't have to pay for girls, no matter what Jeff thinks.

The girl is a bundle of nerves as she holds her elbow and looks around with short, jerky movements. The bidding war starts and my screen keeps lighting up as the hidden billionaires try to outbid each other.

Sarah looks around at the black glass walls as she bites at her lips nervously. The men can see her but she can't see the men.

The auction comes to a halt when there's no more bidders. Sarah's virginity is sold for $800,000 to bidder number six.

The door opens once again and Sarah rushes through it, looking relieved to get the hell out of there.

I shake my head as the door slides shut. This is barbaric. I'm already playing in my head how I'm going to tell Jeff that he's fired. I can't wait to see the look on his face. He's going to earn it for putting me in this horrible situation.

I down the rest of my scotch as the door slides open

again and the next girl to be auctioned is about to come out. Her stats pop up on my screen:

Jessica Evans

Eighteen.

Virgin.

5'5. 122 lbs.

I should just leave. This is not my scene. I should just get the-

My body jolts like I was just hit by a stun gun. She walks out and it's like the ground has been yanked out from under my feet. If I wasn't sitting I would have collapsed to the floor.

She's perfect.

My body tightens and my chest burns as I stare at her with my heart racing. She's the most beautiful thing that I've ever seen and I *must* have her.

A heavy feeling grips my stomach as I stare at her with a dazed look. The need is more than wanting her. I must *own* her.

She's absolutely stunning, standing in the middle of the stage wearing a school girl's outfit. Long brown hair that falls down in waves, framing the prettiest face that I've ever laid eyes on. She looks uncomfortable as she fidgets with the bottom of her plaid skirt that finishes way to high on her soft thighs.

The first thought that cuts through the haze in my head is the need to cover her up. I don't want anyone to see her. Ever.

I explode out of my chair, pacing around the small room like a caged tiger as I stare at her with gritted teeth. Growls and snarls rip from my throat as my eyes dart around to the black walls of glass, each one hiding a pair of eyes that shouldn't be anywhere near my girl. *My Jessica.*

My hands are shaking as I clench them into fists,

wanting to take the eyes of every man who's looking at her. They're stealing her innocence and it's making me crazy.

Her innocence is mine. Mine alone to take.

Jessica's sweet brown eyes drop to her feet as she shifts her weight from foot to foot. She looks so uncomfortable. So exposed.

I desperately want to take her from here where I can keep her safe but I don't know what to do. My thoughts are so fuzzy right now and I can't think. It's not like me. I'm usually so on the ball. So sharp. So composed.

The sight of this girl is breaking my brain.

She turns to me and raises her shining eyes to mine and it nearly ends me. I'm breathless as she looks straight at me with a stunned look. I can see her but she can't see me.

My body feels hypnotized. My skin tingles as my feet move on their own toward the glass. I don't know who's controlling them but it's not me.

She's still staring at me as I walk up to the one-way glass, stopping a few inches from it. I see my own reflection first, looking back at me, only it's not me. I look different. Crazed. Disheveled. Shaky. Desperate.

This obsessed man who is practically panting for this girl can't be me, only it is.

I push past my reflection to look at the Goddess who is causing my body to react like this. Her gorgeous brown eyes are alive and flighty, darting around nervously as her chest rises and falls with quick shallow breaths.

Her white shirt is too revealing. It falls too low, showing off her perfectly round tits and rises too high in a knot, giving me a flash of her flat stomach and heart-stopping belly button.

My face starts to twitch as an edgy feeling consumes me.

The eyes on her, it's driving me mad. I'm overcome with a need to cover her body.

My back is covered in sweat. I feel like I'm losing it as I stare at her, dragging my eyes past her slim hips, down to her smooth legs with the knee high socks that are hot as fuck.

The screen at my feet lights up as the bidding begins and I feel an uncontrollable rage surge through my body at the dead men who are trying to take this beauty from me.

Don't they know that she's already *mine*?

I whip my body around and slam my palm down on the green button, raising the bid. I don't care what she costs me. I don't care if I have to eat garbage and live in a cave for the rest of my life. I just need her by my side and *nothing* is going to stop that from happening.

She shakes out her hands as she takes a deep nervous breath and my pulse starts racing even more. I can't take my eyes off her. I know in that moment that my life will never be the same. She's in it now, whether she knows it or not and my life has a new purpose. My universe revolves around her.

Another bid lights up the screen and my lips curl up as a snarl rips out of my throat. I'll kill anyone who tries to take her from me. They'll die screaming if they think they can touch her.

I pry my eyes off of her for the split second that it takes to smash my hand onto the button, upping the bid by another twenty-five grand.

No matter how many times I hit the button, someone else keeps trying to outbid me. Adrenaline rushes through my veins as I pace around the tiny room, cursing as these dead men keep trying to take her from me. I smash the button again and again and again.

I don't care what the cost of her is. I'll pay every cent that I have until all of my billions are gone and I'm left with nothing but her.

I just want this to be over and have her secure in my arms but these fuckers keep hitting their buttons as well.

I slam back my scotch as the bidding crosses a million dollars. My throat is painfully dry from my rushed breathing. There's a pounding in my ears as I hit the button again.

When the price passes three million dollars, it's only me and bidder number four left fighting for her.

I glare at his window with furious eyes, dreaming of smashing through it and slitting his throat. Any competition to her must be eliminated. I don't care if it's murder. I don't care if it's barbaric. I only care about possessing her completely and anyone who threatens that must be removed from this planet.

The second he bids, I'm smashing my fist down onto the button like a hammer. Every hit of the button makes my rage increase until it's nearly boiling.

When the price crosses four million I hit the green button with so much frustration that it jams.

Pure panic seizes me as the counter counts down from ten. I claw at the button as it crosses *nine, eight, seven*. Each second lost is like a stab of adrenaline to my heart and I start to freak out, punching and kicking the chair, desperately trying to get the button to work.

Six.

Five.

I can't breathe. It's not working.

"Wait!" I scream but the sound just echoes in the sound-proof room, bouncing back into my pounding ears. "*I want her!*"

Four.

Three.

I can't think. My hands start shaking.

The screen turns red as the clock winds down.

Two.

A cold chill rips through me as every worst fear comes crashing down on me. I'm going to lose her.

One.

The price locks on $4,250,000. Bidder number four wins.

My stomach drops as I fall to my knees, feeling like I'm going to puke.

The door behind her slides open and I explode to my feet before she disappears through it and out of my life forever.

I'll die without her. I know because I'll slit my own wrists if I can't live with her by my side.

A guttural roar erupts from my chest as I grab the chair and yank it off the ground. With a savage grunt I smash it into the dark window as hard as I can. It crashes through the glass, smashing the window to pieces.

Jessica screams as she jumps back, jerking her head toward me. Her eyes are wide with shock as her trembling hand flies up to cover her open mouth.

I charge through the broken glass onto the lit up stage as she gapes up at me with the most striking brown eyes that I've ever seen. She's even more flawless in real life without the darkness of the glass muting her beauty.

We just stare at each other like two souls who are finally seeing their other half for the first time. There are no words that can be said to describe what I'm feeling.

My chest is burning, my head spinning, but I dig down deep for her.

"I'm taking you."

She swallows hard as she looks up at me with a soft expression on her face. My heart nearly explodes when she nods.

"I've been waiting for you." Her voice is better than any song I've ever heard. Sweeter than any candy I've tasted. Each soft word cuts through me and strums on my soul, making my chest swell up.

Without a second of hesitation I grab her and toss her over my shoulder. She moans as I grip the back of her soft thigh with my hand and turn back to the broken window.

Bidder number four is banging his fists on his window in an outrage. He better hope that the glass doesn't break because I'll end his life before the shattered pieces hit the ground.

I'd love to go and take care of him now but the girl on my shoulder is my top concern.

I need to get her out of here. I need to get her to safety.

I need to get her to *my room*.

And that's exactly where I'm going.

I grit my teeth and run.

Made in the USA
Columbia, SC
21 June 2023